This book
belongs to:

Or would you go to the city, be friends

fountain in it, travel by rickshaw, eat lo

and a deerstalker hat, keep a pet touca

for fun and sleep in a bunk bed? Or wo

ghost, live in a wigwam with a trampolir

and beans, wear a denim jacket with a ti

fashion model, blow bubbles and sl

the beach, be friends with a Viking, liv

in it, travel by limousine, eat a box of ch

hat and fluffy mules, keep a pet elephan

and sleep in a kennel? Or would you go t

an apartment with a secret door in it, tr

a poncho with stilettos and a furry hc

line dancing and sleep on a cot? Or v

be friends with an alien, live in a ligl

canoe, eat a bag of chips, wear a kil

a pet unicorn, be an astronaut, do

with a pirate, live in a spaceship with a
ster, wear a suit of armor with sneakers
, be a deep-sea diver, build a snowman
ld you go to the moon, be friends with a
in it, travel by paddle boat, eat sausages
ra and wedges, keep a pet monkey, be a
ep in a shoe? Or would you go to
in a fairy palace with a ping-pong table
colates, wear a grass skirt with a cowboy
, be a hairdresser, go on a bouncy castle
a desert, be friends with a knight, live in
vel by helicopter, eat a hamburger, wear
, keep a pet spider, be a magician, go
uld you go to the top of a mountain,
house with chandeliers in it, travel by
with rain boots and a sombrero, keep
a jigsaw and sleep in a hammock?

In memory of Henry Brown
N. S.

To everyone at Browsers Bookshop
P. G.

First American Edition 2012
Kane Miller, A Division of EDC Publishing

First published in Great Britain in 2003
This edition published by permission of
Random House Children's Books, London
Text © Pippa Goodhart, 2003
Illustration © Nick Sharratt, 2003

Library of Congress Control Number: 2011931493

Printed and bound in China
1 2 3 4 5 6 7 8 9 10
ISBN: 978-1-61067-076-0

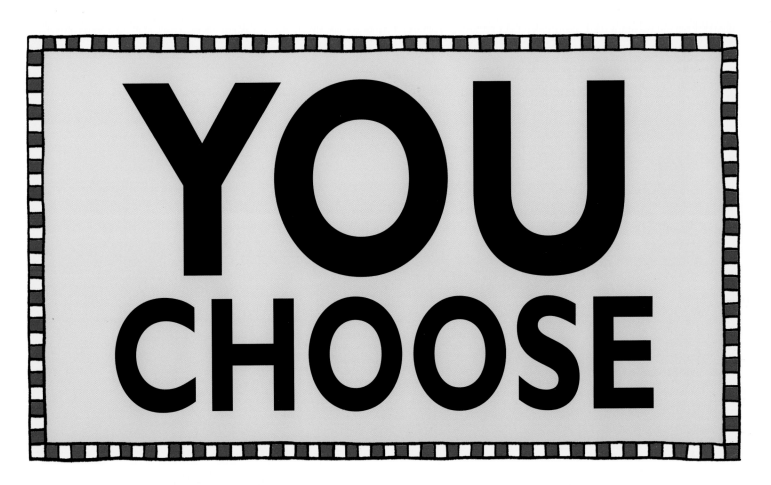

Words by Pippa Goodhart, pictures by Nick Sharratt

Kane Miller
A DIVISION OF EDC PUBLISHING

If you could go anywhere,

where would you go?

family and friends?

What kind of home

would you choose?

Would you travel with wheels or wings?

Or perhaps choose one of these other things?

what would you eat?

Choose some shoes ...

...and perhaps a hat?

Why not get yourself a pet...

or two or three or more?

Is there a job

you'd like to to do?

What would you do...

...for fun?

And when you got tired and felt like a snooze,

where would you sleep? You choose. Good night!

Or would you go to the desert, be frie
with a **drum set** in it, travel by **airship**, ea
flops and a **furry hat**, keep a pet
for fun and sleep in a **cradle**? Or would y
live in a **cave** with a **swimming pool** in
wear a **tuxedo** with **Roman sandals** and a b
on a **roller coaster** and sleep in a
outer space, be friends with a **baby**,
on it, travel by **steam train**, eat a **waterm**
lacy boots, keep a pet **polar bear**,
and sleep in a **hammock**? Or would you
live in a **cottage** with a **secret door** in it,
wear a **kilt** with **clogs** and a top h
bird-watching and sleep in a **nest**? Or
be friends with a **vampire**, live in a **treeh**
space shuttle, eat **squid**, wear a **bow tie**
a pet **bat**, be a **deep-sea diver**, rea